Hello, Family Members,

Learning to read is one of the most important accomplishments of early childhood. **Hello Reader!** books are designed to help children become skilled readers who like to read. Beginning readers learn to read by remembering frequently used words like "the," "is," and "and"; by using phonics skills to decode new words; and by interpreting picture and text clues. These books provide both the stories children enjoy and the structure they need to read fluently and independently. Here are suggestions for helping your child *before, during,* and *after* reading:

Before

- Look at the cover and pictures and have your child predict what the story is about.
- Read the story to your child.
- Encourage your child to chime in with familiar words and phrases.
- Echo read with your child by reading a line first and having your child read it after you do.

During

- Have your child think about a word he or she does not recognize right away. Provide hints such as "Let's see if we know the sounds" and "Have we read other words like this one?"
- Encourage your child to use phonics skills to sound out new words.
- Provide the word for your child when more assistance is needed so that he or she does not struggle and the experience of reading with you is a positive one.
- Encourage your child to have fun by reading with a lot of expression . . . like an actor!

After

- Have your child keep lists of interesting and favorite words.
- Encourage your child to read the books over and over again. Have him or her read to brothers, sisters, grandparents, and even teddy bears. Repeated readings develop confidence in young readers.
- Talk about the stories. Ask and answer questions. Share ideas about the funniest and most interesting characters and events in the stories.

I do hope that you and your child enjoy this book.

—Francie Alexander
Chief Education Officer,
Scholastic Education

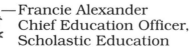

To Jordan
— Love, Mommy

For Edie Weinberg
— B.L.

**Go to www.scholastic.com for Web site information
on Scholastic authors and illustrators.**

Text copyright © 1999 by Grace Maccarone.
Illustrations copyright © 1999 by Betsy Lewin.
All rights reserved. Published by Scholastic Inc.
SCHOLASTIC, HELLO READER, CARTWHEEL BOOKS
and associated logos are trademarks and/or registered
trademarks of Scholastic Inc.

Library of Congress Cataloging-in-Publication Data

Maccarone, Grace.
    The class trip / by Grace Maccarone; illustrated by Betsy Lewin.
        p.   cm. — (First grade friends) (Hello reader! Level 1)
    "Cartwheel Books."
    Summary: When his class goes to the zoo, Sam fails to keep up with the rest of the group and gets lost.
    ISBN 0-439-06755-3
    [1. Zoos — Fiction.   2. Zoo animals — Fiction.   3. School field trips — Fiction.   4. Lost children — Fiction.   5. Stories in rhyme.]
    I. Lewin, Betsy, ill.   II. Title.   III. Series.   IV. Series: Maccarone, Grace. First grade friends.
    PZ8.3.M127Cj   1999   99-10687
    [E]—dc21   CIP
                                                                                                      AC

10 9 8 7 6 5 4 3 2 1   02 03 04 05 06

Printed in Singapore   46
This edition first printing, October 2002

The Class Trip

by Grace Maccarone
Illustrated by Betsy Lewin

Hello Reader! — Level 1

SCHOLASTIC INC.
New York Toronto London Auckland Sydney
Mexico City New Delhi Hong Kong Buenos Aires

Cartwheel
B·O·O·K·S·®

The teacher says,
"It's time to go."
So she puts on her hat
with the polka-dot bow.

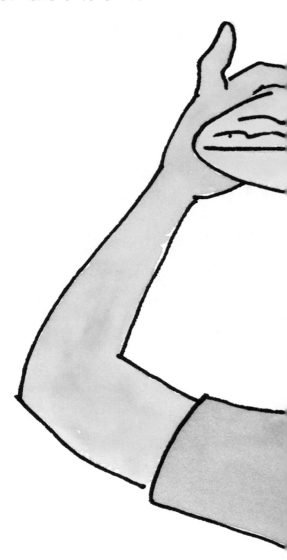

Then Sam, Jan, Pam,
Max, Kim, and Dan

get on the bus
as fast as they can.

They sit in seats
two by two.
They talk. They sing.

They're at the zoo.

Sam sees the chimps.
They fight. They play.

Sam's friends move on.
Sam wants to stay.

The teacher says,
"Sam, don't be slow.
Keep up with the group.
It's time to go."

Monkeys chatter.
They swing. They climb.

Sam is having
a wonderful time.

The teacher says,
"Sam, don't be slow.
Keep up with the group.
It's time to go."

Elephants walk.

Lions run.

Polar bears
enjoy the sun.
Sam is having
so much fun.

The teacher says,
"Sam, don't be slow.
Keep up with the group.
It's time to go."

Fish swim.

Frogs leap.

Flowers float.

Turtles sleep.

Sam looks up
and has a scare.
Sam is alone.
His group is not there!

Which way did they go?
Sam does not know.
He looks up high.
He looks down low.
Sam tries to stand
on tippy-toe.

And that's when he sees
the polka-dot bow.
Sam runs to his teacher.

Now he will know
to stay with his group
and go, go, go, GO!

The Classroom Pet

To Betsy Lewin
— G.M.

To Seraphina Dilcher
— B.L.

Text copyright © 1995 by Grace Maccarone.
Illustrations copyright © 1995 by Betsy Lewin.
All rights reserved. Published by Scholastic Inc.
SCHOLASTIC, HELLO READER, CARTWHEEL BOOKS, and associated
logos are trademarks and/or registered trademarks of Scholastic Inc.

Library of Congress Cataloging-in-Publication Data

Maccarone, Grace.
   The classroom pet / by Grace Maccarone ; illustrated by Betsy
Lewin.
      p.   cm. — (Hello reader! Level 1)
   "Cartwheel Books."
   Summary: Sam is in charge of taking care of the classroom hermit
crab over Christmas vacation, but when he turns his back, the crab
disappears.
   ISBN 0-590-26264-5
   [1. Hermit crabs — Fiction.   2. Crabs — Fiction   3. Schools —
Fiction.   4. Stories in rhyme.]   I. Lewin, Betsy, ill.   II. Title.   III.
Series.   IV. Series : Maccarone, Grace.   First grade friends
PZ8.3.M127Cl   1995
[E] — dc20   95-13151
                                                                      CIP
                                                                       AC

The Classroom Pet

by Grace Maccarone
Illustrated by Betsy Lewin

Hello Reader! — Level 1

SCHOLASTIC INC.
New York Toronto London Auckland Sydney
Mexico City New Delhi Hong Kong Buenos Aires

It's the day
before Christmas...
It's almost three.
The class is sitting quietly
to hear who gets
the classroom pets.

The snake goes home with Kim.

The rabbit goes with Dan.

The ant farm goes with Max.

The hamster goes with Jan.

Sam gets the crab.
Her name is Star.

Oops! Star falls down
in Mommy's car.

Sam gives Star water.
Sam gives Star bread.

Sam says good night
and goes to bed.

Sam wakes up
to something great.
Star is eating
from her plate.

In the kitchen,
Sam lets Star crawl
across the floor,
along the wall.

Sam turns around
to get a pear.
When Sam turns back,
Star is *not* there!

Where is Star?
Where did she go?
Sam looks high.

Sam looks low —

under the bed,

under a chair,

with the toys.

No! Not in there!

Sam wants to cry.
Where could Star be?
Now Sam sees
the Christmas tree!

Then Sam takes back
the classroom pet.
And this is a story
that Sam won't forget.

The Gym Day Winner

To Steve
— G.M.

To Grant Geary
— B.L.

I would like to thank Betsy Molisani and her wonderful first-grade class, Coach Connolly, and Edward Kennedy for letting me go to school with them.

— Grace Maccarone

Text copyright © 1996 by Grace Maccarone
Illustrations copyright © 1996 by Betsy Lewin
All rights reserved. Published by Scholastic Inc.
SCHOLASTIC, HELLO READER, CARTWHEEL BOOKS, and associated logos are trademarks and/or registered trademarks of Scholastic Inc.

Library of Congress Cataloging-in-Publication Data

Maccarone, Grace.
    The gym day winner / by Grace Maccarone ; illustrated by Betsy Lewin.
        p.   cm. — (First-grade friends) (Hello reader! Level 1)
    "Cartwheel Books."
    Summary: During gym at school, Sam always comes in last, but a great basketball shot turns him into the hero of the day.
    ISBN 0-590-26263-7
    [1. Basketball — Fiction. 2. Schools — Fiction] I. Lewin, Betsy, ill. II. Title. III. Series. IV. Series : Maccarone, Grace. First grade friends
PZ7.M127Gy   1996
[E] — dc20   95-10285
                                                CIP
                                                AC

The Gym Day Winner

by Grace Maccarone
Illustrated by Betsy Lewin

Hello Reader! — Level 1

SCHOLASTIC INC.   Cartwheel B·O·O·K·S·®
New York   Toronto   London   Auckland   Sydney
Mexico City   New Delhi   Hong Kong   Buenos Aires

It's Thursday.
It is time for gym
for Dan, Jan, Pam,
Sam, Max, and Kim.

Max tags Pam.

Pam tags Dan.

Dan tags Kim.

Kim tags Jan.

But Jan and Kim,
Dan, Max, and Pam —
all of them —
are tagging Sam.

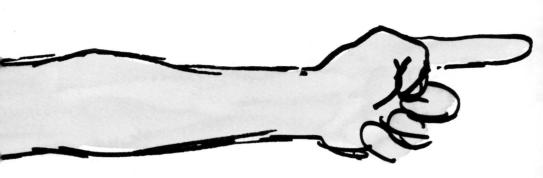

Coach Mike is big
and strong and fun.
He blows his whistle.
He says, "Let's run!"

The children race.
Dan is fast.

Pam is faster.

Sam is last.

Now Jan does cartwheels.
Kim does flips.

Max does rolls.

Sam just trips.

Coach Mike shouts out,
"Go into groups
for three-on-three.
It's time for hoops!"

The children dribble,
pass, and run.

They shoot. They miss.
They're having fun.

Now Dan has two kids
guarding him —
both Pam and Max —

and Jan guards Kim.

But no one guards Sam
because Sam is not fast.
No one guards Sam
because Sam's always last.

Now Dan must pass.
He's in a jam.
Dan throws the ball.

It goes to Sam!

Sam takes a shot.

The ball goes in.
Hooray for Sam!
His team will win.

The Lunch Box Surprise

To Betsy Molisani—Thanks
for the lunch!
—G.M.

To Angie "Nana" Cosentino
—B.L.

Text copyright © 1995 by Grace Maccarone.
Illustrations copyright © 1995 by Betsy Lewin.
All rights reserved. Published by Scholastic Inc.
SCHOLASTIC, HELLO READER, CARTWHEEL BOOKS, and associated
logos are trademarks and/or registered trademarks of Scholastic Inc.

Library of Congress Cataloging-in-Publication Data

Maccarone, Grace.
    The lunch box surprise / by Grace Maccarone ; illustrated by Betsy Lewin.
        p.   cm. — (First grade friends ; bk. 1) (Hello reader! Level 1)
    "Cartwheel Books."
    Summary: When Sam's mother forgets to pack his lunch, his friends in the
first grade come to his rescue.
    ISBN 0-590-26267-X
    [1. Schools — Fiction.   2. Friendship — Fiction.]   I. Lewin, Betsy, ill.
II. Title.   III. Series.   IV. Series: Maccarone, Grace. First grade friends ;
bk. 1.
PZ7.M1257Lu   1995   95-10284
[E]—dc20   CIP
                                                                                 AC

The Lunch Box Surprise

by Grace Maccarone
Illustrated by Betsy Lewin

Hello Reader! — Level 1

SCHOLASTIC INC. Cartwheel B·O·O·K·S ®
New York Toronto London Auckland Sydney
Mexico City New Delhi Hong Kong Buenos Aires

"It's time for lunch.
It's time to eat,"
the teacher says.
"Now take your seat!"

"My lunch is best,"
say Jan and Pam

and Kim and Dan

and Max and Sam.

Jan has peanut butter,
bread, and jam.

Pam has soup.

Dan has ham.

Kim has tuna,
toast, and cheese.

Max has chicken,
rice, and peas.

But Sam has nothing—
not a spot.
Sam has nothing!
His mom forgot!

Sam is surprised.
Sam is sad.
Sam is hungry.
Sam is mad!

But Max and Kim,
Jan, Dan, and Pam
feel sorry
for their sad friend, Sam.

Jan gives Sam
peanut butter,
bread, and jam.

Pam gives him soup.
Dan gives him ham.

Kim gives him tuna,
toast, and cheese.

Max gives him chicken, rice, and peas.

Now Sam is not sad
and Sam is not mad.
This is the best lunch
Sam ever had!

Recess Mess

To Gina Shaw,
who spells very well
— G.M.

To Samuel Gus Ziebel
and Jordan Emily Zwetchkenbaum
— B.L.

Text copyright © 1996 by Grace Maccarone.
Illustrations copyright © 1996 by Betsy Lewin.
All rights reserved. Published by Scholastic Inc.
SCHOLASTIC, HELLO READER, CARTWHEEL BOOKS, and associated
logos are trademarks and/or registered trademarks of Scholastic Inc.

Library of Congress Cataloging-in-Publication Data

Maccarone, Grace.
    Recess mess / by Grace Maccarone; illustrated by Betsy Lewin.
      p.   cm. — (First-grade friends) (Hello reader! Level 1)
    Summary: First-grade boys and girls go out to play at recess.
    ISBN 0-590-73878-X
    [1. Play — Fiction. 2. Schools — Fiction. 3. Stories in rhyme.]
    I. Lewin, Betsy, ill. II. Title. III. Series. IV. Series:
    Maccarone, Grace. First-grade friends.
  PZ8.3.M217Re   1996
[E] — dc20   95-36016
                                                              CIP
                                                               AC

Recess Mess

by Grace Maccarone
Illustrated by Betsy Lewin

Hello Reader! — Level 1

Cartwheel
·B·O·O·K·S·®

SCHOLASTIC INC.
New York   Toronto   London   Auckland   Sydney
Mexico City   New Delhi   Hong Kong   Buenos Aires

Sam, Dan, Pam,
Kim, Max, and Jan
put away books
as fast as they can.

They put on coats.

They get in line.

They go outside.
It's recess time.

Dan runs.

Pam rolls.

Max slides.

Kim crawls.

Jan climbs.

Sam swings.

Sam swings.

Sam falls.

Dan throws. Pam catches.

Jan dances. Max hops.

Kim skips.

Sam jumps.

Sam jumps. Sam stops.

Sam looks for the boys' room.
He needs to go.
He sees two doors.
But wait! Oh, no!
Sam never used
this room before.
Sam tries to read
what's on the door.

B-O-Y?
G-I-R-L?
But Sam can't read.
And Sam can't spell.

What should Sam do?
Which should Sam use?
Sam gets an idea
to help him choose.

Sam will wait
and wait some more
for a boy or a girl
to come out of the door.

Now Sam is happy.
Sam feels swell.
He knows how to read
and he knows how to spell—

B-O-Y and G-I-R-L.

First-Grade Friends

Sharing Time Troubles

To Michelle, who still has lots of hop
— G.M.

To Samuel Gus Ziebel
and Jordan Emily Zwetchkenbaum
— B.L.

Text copyright © 1997 by Grace Maccarone.
Illustrations copyright © 1997 by Betsy Lewin.
All rights reserved. Published by Scholastic Inc.
SCHOLASTIC, HELLO READER, CARTWHEEL BOOKS, and associated logos
are trademarks and/or registered trademarks of Scholastic Inc.

Library of Congress Cataloging-in-Publication Data

Maccarone, Grace.
    Sharing time troubles / by Grace Maccarone; illustrated by Betsy Lewin.
      p.   cm. — (First-grade friends) (Hello reader! Level 1)
    Summary: Sam searches through all of his toys but can't find anything
good enough to take to school for show and tell until his troublesome little
brother appears.
    ISBN 0-590-73879-8
    [1. Sharing — Fiction. 2. Brothers — Fiction. 3. Schools — Fiction.
4. Stories in rhyme.]
    I. Lewin, Betsy, ill. II. Title. III. Series. IV. Series:
    Maccarone, Grace. First-grade friends.
PZ8.3.M217Sh   1997
[E] — dc20   95-36015
                                          CIP
                                          AC

First-Grade Friends

Sharing Time Troubles

by Grace Maccarone
Illustrated by Betsy Lewin

Hello Reader! — Level 1

SCHOLASTIC INC.
New York   Toronto   London   Auckland   Sydney
Mexico City   New Delhi   Hong Kong   Buenos Aires

It's Monday.
It is sharing time.

Dan brings his pet,
a frog named Slime.

It's Tuesday.
It is time to share.
Pam brings her special
Teddy bear.

On Wednesday, Max brings Mexican money.

Kim brings gold.

Jan brings
a bunny.

On Thursday,
Sam has nothing to share.
No pet. No gold.
No money. No bear.

At home, Sam looks
at all his stuff.
But none of it
is good enough.

Books, blocks, balls,
a baseball bat.
Cards and caps,
a cowboy hat.

Sam's little brother
wants to play.

But Sam has sharing time troubles today.
Sam says, "Go away."

Then Sam says, "Stay!"

It's Friday, and Sam
has something to show.
"Can you guess what it is?"
Sam asks. "Do you know—

what's as sloppy as a frog,

as hoppy as a bunny,

as cute as a Teddy bear,
and better than gold or money?"

Jan makes a guess.
Dan makes another.
"I know!" says Kim.

"It's Sam's little brother!"